Worlds of Science Fiction and Fantasy

Russ Crossley
with R.G. Hart

53RD STREET PUBLISHING

Worlds of Science Fiction and Fantasy

Published by 53rd Street Publishing

ISBN 978-1-927621-19-6

Table of Contents

Introduction

This collection of five stories reflects the kinds of stories I love. Science fiction about other worlds and cultures, fantasy about ghosts and pirates, and two people thrown together by danger and adventure who discover they share a mutual attraction.

In these stories you will discover a planet for sale, and doorways to other times and worlds where ordinary people like you and I face an unknown future. Warriors who face life and death decisions that will test their courage to the limit and beyond.

I hope you enjoy these stories and hope these characters will speak to you as they did me when I wrote about them.

Russ Crossley
March 2012
Vancouver, Canada

Lock, Stock, and Barrel

Simon grunted as he dropped to his knees on the dusty shop floor. His knees cracked and a sharp pain pinched his lower back. Simon Pyman felt older than dirt.

He squinted at the damaged heel in the poor light.

Lying on his stomach he thumbed the button on the flashlight in his left hand and a cone of white light illuminated the back of Shapiro's foot. He knew he should buy stronger light bulbs, but since he's a cheap man he didn't.

The simulacrum stood like a statue as Simon peered closely at the tear in the plasti-skin. It seemed sim's were always breaking down. His hazel eyes narrowed. "There it is," he muttered.

Using his index finger Simon pulled out the damaged wire from the tear in the sim's plasti-skin.

Shapiro must've caught his foot on something to tear a hole this big. It wasn't surprising to him Shapiro was having trouble given the size of the tear. Wires don't take kindly to Windmill's rainy, cold weather.

He eyed the hole and saw rain water had collected inside the tear at the bottom of the heel like a cup.

"Wally?" he said glancing over this shoulder at his assistant Wally Ogdon seated on a molded plastic chair near the work bench across the cluttered workshop. In his greasy hands Wally held a sandwich comprised of two slices of white bread, mayonnaise, and cloned cheese. Wally ate the same thing every day since he started as assistant mechanic. He wasn't much of a mechanic, but Simon couldn't be too choosy given there were very few humans left of the original colonists. Not that Wally himself was an original. He came later.

Wally looked up from studying his meal, his sea green eyes questioning. "Yeah, boss?"

Simon chuckled. "How many times do I have to tell you not to call me boss? My name's Simon." As if telling him for the millionth time is going to change anything. Wally's eyes drooped.

"Never mind," he said cringing. Wally was too sensitive for his own good.

"Sorry. Bring me the soldering gun will you? Shapiro needs a tune up."

"Looks like he stepped in a rabbit hole to me," said Wally with a shrug. He stood, placed his sandwich on a plain brown wrapper on the workbench, then went to retrieve the soldering gun from the cubbyhole above the bench where Simon kept it.

Wally walked toward him cradling the tool in his pale hands as if it were a baby. He's going to make a good nurse someday.

After handing Simon the soldering gun Wally dropped to his haunches and peered at the damage to the sim's foot.

"There're no rabbits on Windmill," said Simon. His eyes crinkled at the corners. "But you know that."

Wally's mouth formed a thin smile and he blew at a lock of carrot-colored hair that had fallen across his face. "Kilroy rats are kinda like rabbits."

Simon shifted his gaze back to the task at hand and brought the tip of the soldering gun closer to the wire. "Rabbits with razor sharp teeth aren't rabbits."

Pressing the trigger on the gun caused the tip to become white hot, while at the same producing a stream of liquid metal that coated the wire. "There," he said with satisfaction. "One more thing and we're done."

He handed the soldering gun to Wally who carried it to the bench and returned with a small plastic packet containing white powder. He handed it to Simon.

A bell sounded coming from the direction of the reception counter at the front of the shop. Simon closed his eyes and sighed. What now? I'm just about done.

"Go see who it is," he said to Wally.

"Okay, boss." He heard Wally's shuffling foot steps as he left to see who was at reception.

After his assistant was gone he opened his eyes and studied the tear in the plasti-skin. About three ounces should do it.

He pulled the zip lock across the top of the packet then poured a small pile of the powder on the shop floor. The smell of vanilla emanating from the powder filled his nostrils. That looks about right.

"Hey, boss," said Wally startling him. He sneezed and the powder blew away.

"Wally!"

"Oops. Sorry, boss."

Simon's next words were going to be you're fired, but he knew he couldn't fire him, he liked Wally too much.

"A guy out front really wants to talk to you."

"A guy? And?" Simon got off the floor using his hands to brush shop dust and the remnants of the plasti-skin repair compound off his coveralls.

"And he's a real estate guy."

A knot formed in Simon's belly. Someone had finally answered the ad.

"Ok." Simon paused. He had to remain cool. He didn't want to look as anxious as a virgin bride on her wedding night. "Good."

He buried his trembling hands in the long pockets of his coveralls. "What's he look like?"

"I don't know." Wally's pale forehead wrinkled. "A guy. Tall, thin, wearing a fancy suit, and his shoes look expensive. Antrim lizard skin I'd say."

He stared at his assistant. "Whoa, have you been watching the fashion vids again?"

Wally smirked. "I wasn't always a mechanic's assistant."

Slapping Wally on his shoulder Simon laughed. "Of course not. How's about we catch Suz's show at the Ol' Miner one day after work and you tell me all about it."

"Sure," he shrugged. "Why not?"

"Why don't you finish fixing ol' Shapiro here and I'll go talk to the real estate guy. Sound good?"

"Sure."

When Simon entered the lobby the man Wally described was seated in the cloned leather chair next to the glass door. What Wally neglected to tell him the guy wasn't human, even if he wore human clothes. The blue skin of the back of his hands looked rough to the touch. He's a Thom.

Thom's reputation as the ultimate salesmen in the galaxy is well known, even on the outer rim worlds like Windmill. And Windmill is the farthest planet from the galactic core.

Alien or human he was just grateful someone finally responded to his ad.

Thom's don't shake hands so Simon was grateful he could keep his hands buried in his pockets. "Hi. Can I help you?"

The Thom stood up and Simon realized Wally wasn't exaggerating. He was a bigun alright, must be at least a seven footer.

"Mr. Pyman?" Simon smiled and nodded. "My name's Cinder Burns." He reached into the inside pocket of his grey suit jacket and pulled out a business card which he offered to Simon.

Simon pulled his right hand out of the pocket of his coveralls, pleased to see it had stopped shaking, and accept the card.

His bladder screamed when he read Cinder Burns name over the title UNISERVE COLLECTION AGENCY. That's one of Andre Champions shell companies. He quickly stuffed his hand back in his pocket when it began to tremble.

"What can I do for you?"

The Thom smiled making Simon slightly queasy. When a Thom smiles its lips roll back to reveal its purple gums and double rows of yellow teeth. Burns said, "I represent an interested buyer."

Suppressing his revulsion Simon pocketed Burns' card and then crossed his arms over his chest and leaned his lean frame against the wall. He frowned. "What does this buyer want to pay for the planet?"

The Thom blew air from its single nasal hole in the middle of its face between the mouth and the black eyes. "The buyer wishes to buy you."

"Me?" Simon straightened. "I thought this is about my ad."

"Ad?"

"Yes. I'm selling the planet lock, stock and barrel."

"The planet?" Burns emitted a mixture of growl, groan and guffaw throwing his large hairless head back in the process.

He had never heard a Thom laugh before. At least he hoped it was laughter. It sounded more like a cow in heat.

"No, Mr. Pyman. I'm sorry but the buyer's not interested in the planet. After the failure of the colony and the Terra forming project twenty six years ago no one is interested in this property." Burns approached the counter. Simon's nose wrinkled and resisted the urge to take a step back and pinch his nose. A Thom's breath reeks of sour milk.

"We have minerals," said Simon matter-of-factly. "The sims discovered a vein of lime quartz just the other day."

The Thom laughed again turned and headed for the front door. Through the glass door Simon saw the glittering rain that fell in sheets from the billowing clouds that crowded the sky day and night.

Rain. It always rains. What was he thinking? Only a duck would buy this planet.

He glanced at the digital clock on the wall to the left of the door. It was almost closing time.

"Think about it, Mr. Pyman." Burns pushed against the aluminum bar across the door but stopped after it opened part way and swiveled his head to gaze at Simon. "Simon Pyman?" he shook his head in a very human manner.

"Really? A nursery rhyme? Bit simple don't you think?"

After Burns disappeared into the gathering gloom Simon took a deep breath. He's a bounty hunter. They knew where he was. Now what is he going to do?

***

After he sent Wally home for the day he hurried to his apartment over Rosie's Bar and Grill. He even hired an air taxi, unusual given the cost and his modest income from the shop.

Seated behind the plasti-steel desk his finger tips brushed the hidden button under the desk top. He rolled his chair back pushing with his feet as the desk top swung upward to reveal a thin, flat screen. Within milliseconds the screen lit up to reveal a smiling blonde woman.

"Yes, darling?" said the image. Today she wore his favorite ruby red spaghetti strap cocktail dress. His mouth formed a wry smile. He'd grown to love this new interface with his AI. Wally was a genius with AI's.

He pulled his chair forward with his feet until his stomach bumped against the edge of the desk. The blue eyed blonde gazed at him with a loving expression on her angular features.

"Hey, Jill. I need transportation. Fast."

"I will summon a taxi, sweetie. Fast." Jill's tone was edged with disappointment.

"No, Jill!" He knew his nerves were really on edge. Stupid. "Sorry, Jill. I didn't mean local transportation. I mean off planet. I mean out of system. I mean anywhere in the galaxy BUT here, and as soon as possible, preferably sooner."

"Is there a problem, lovey?" Jill purred and her perfect digital mouth formed a sensual pout.

"Of course not, Jill my love I just received an e-gram from my aunt saying my favorite uncle left me a Monastery on Zebra II and I want to collect is all."

"I don't recall any e-gram, darling." Now she sounded like a little girl.

"No. Wally went to check the public boards for me and brought it to me."

"But, huny bun —"

"Never mind, Jill, it doesn't matter," Simon cut her off. "Have you found me transportation?" AI's were capable of processing forty-seven billion terabytes of data simultaneously. Jill could solve the riddles of the universe, seduce him, check his mail, and hopefully find him a way off Windmill all within milliseconds.

"Yes. The Marketeer FTL ship Moby Dick currently in orbit is scheduled to depart at 0640 tomorrow morning. It has three passenger spaces available for purchase." Jill paused. Simon frowned. She must think he was going to yell at her again.

"Do you wish me to book passage, Simon?"

Burns must expect to have him in custody by the time that ship leaves. And live probably wasn't a condition of his contract. "No. Thank you, Jill, but no."

He eased back in the chair and thought for a second. One eyebrow arched on his forehead. He was afraid to ask. "Is there anything else? Any other ship?"

"According to the galactic ship masters records there is no vessel scheduled to arrive at Windmill for the next two solar years."

Simon slumped in his chair. That was it, he was sunk. Burns will take him back to Telex Two and Andre Champions goons will tear him up.

He stood and walked to the window over looking the street. The rain had stopped and the clouds had parted after months of steady rain. The twin moons appeared in the western sky to cast a soft white glow over the street scene below.

Various Sims walked past carrying purchases for their owners while some worker sims, still in their rain coats, used shovels to dig mud out of the gutters by the side of the road.

He should never have let Max convince him to steal from Champion. Gangsters don't like it when you rob them. Even if it's the perfect crime. He sighed and watched Shapiro come into view. The simulacrum had a small teacup sized dog tethered on a leash. The dog's eyes were hidden by long fur that covered its tiny body and dragged on the ground. The hair waved like a curtain of hair in time to its bouncy step.

That gives me an idea.

Walking back to the desk he sat down and gazed into Jill's patient azure pools. "Jill, who can create a simulacrum?"

She hesitated. "Be more specific, please."

"Sorry." He rolled his eyes. He was saying sorry a lot lately. "I mean a sim of an actual human."

The perfectly smooth skin of Jill's brow furrowed slightly. "That procedure is illegal, Simon. The Galactic Senate outlawed human copying in 4213."

Since when is she a lawyer? "Yes, I know, Jill but if I wanted a simulacrum of me for say a week or so where would I get it?"

Without hesitation Jill said, "There is one black market dealer currently on Windmill." There was a hint of disapproval in her tone. But who cares what an AI thinks?

"Show me the address." His eyes widened when it appeared on the screen.

That's my shop.

***

Wally's apartment on Monitor Street is on the top floor of a four story brick walk-up. The outside looked like one of those ancient brick buildings he'd seen in history books, only these bricks were constructed from a carbon/titanium/steel/diamond alloy harder than steel. Wally's building dated back eighty years to the first colonist's arrival on Windmill.

He's going to give me some answers, and he's going to build him a sim before morning. Simon looked both ways on the dark street. No sign of Burns. His stomach muscles tightened. It felt like a net was closing in around him.

Pulling back the sleeve of his rain coat he looked at the watch on his wrist. 0043. Time is definitely running out.

His heart pounded in his chest as he raced up the stairs until he finally stood outside apartment 402. There were only two apartments on the top floor.

Wally could never afford this apartment on the salary he paid him. He assumed he made extra money upgrading AI's. He never would have thought his assistant traded in black market tech.

Still breathing hard he pressed his hand on the touch panel recessed into the wall next to the door frame. After several seconds of waiting a simulacrum opened the door. Tall, with oil black hair the male sim looked at Simon as if he were an insect. "We do not accept deliveries outside business hours," he said in a clipped tone.

"Never mind that crap," Simon gasped his hand resting against the door frame, "I need to see Wally Ogdon," he paused to take in a deep breath, "right now."

"I'm sorry but the Master is not receiving visitors at this hour. Please come back later." Simon stuck his foot between the door and the frame.

Simon winced when the sim closed the door on his foot. "Listen, I'm Wally's boss. If he doesn't see me immediately you tell him he's fired. Got it?"

The sim eyed him through the gap between the door and the frame and arched an eyebrow. "One moment, sir." It walked away leaving the door open.

Simon peered through the partially open door and saw very expensive furniture inside. The black market sim business must be good. His eyes locked on what could only be a real leather couch. He whistled softy. Correction. Very, *very* good.

He almost fell when the door suddenly swung open. Wally ran his pale fingers through his unruly orange hair yawning. "Sorry, boss. Jackson's manners are terrible. Com'on in." He stepped back and Simon walked into the apartment.

"Have a seat on the couch," he waved in the direction of the leather couch. "Ya wanta beer?"

"Huh, no. Thanks." Simon smiled thinly. He moved to the couch and sank into the soft cushion.

Wally shrugged, waved the sim away, then shuffled to the matching leather chair opposite the couch his slippers shushing across the thick rug. The sim disappeared into a hallway leading off the living room.

Simon cleared his throat. "Wally, why have you been using the shop for your black market business?"

"Why have you been using the name Simon Pyman?"

Simon felt his cheeks grow warm. "Why not? It's my name."

Wally chuckled and eased back in the chair his arms flat on the chair arms. "No, it's not. Mr. Abram Shakespeare, former resident of Telex Two, and former hired gun for one Mr. Andre Champion."

How does he know? Simon's face paled and his hands began to tremble. Wally might be another bounty hunter.

As if reading his mind Wally added, "Don't worry I'm not a bounty hunter." He stood and walked to the fridge. He opened the door and pulled two brown beer bottles from the slot in the door. He popped the tops with his thumbs. "I'm a mechanic just like you." He walked over and handed Simon one of the beers. "Among other things."

"I don't know what you're talking about." When in doubt deny.

Wally shook his head then walked to the window. His eyes narrowed as he looked out then tipped back the bottle and took a long swig.

The bottle felt cold in Simon's hand. "Alright, Wally let's assume you know who I am. Where do we go from here?" His chances of him building him a sim had evaporated.

Wally shrugged. "What ya got to trade?"

"Trade? For what?"

Wally turned away from the window and shuffled back across the thick carpet. The chair sighed as he sat down. His green eyes were hard as stone, his lips a thin line. The beer bottle was pressed between his hands.

"A one way ticket to a planet so far away Champions people will never find you."

Simon felt beads of sweat tickle his back. "How far is that exactly?" If they found me on Windmill there is no place in the galaxy far enough to hide from Andre Champion.

Wally smirked then raised the bottle to his lips and took a sip. "Too far."

Simon sat forward on the couch until he was on the edge of the cushion. "What do I have to do?"

A slow smile formed on Wally's features. "Trade me Windmill."

Windmill? Is he kidding? Simon had been trying to dump this worthless hunk of rock ever since he won it a poker game fifteen years ago.

A sound of an air taxi's engine from the direction of the street outside made Simon tense. "Ok," he said fighting the desperation in his voice. "When can I leave?"

"Right now." Wally stood and walked to a door that until now Simon thought was a closet.

He opened it.

Shielding his eyes with his hands from the sudden bright light Simon shot to his feet. "Is that what I think it is?"

"Yup. I traded a simulacrum for it with a guy who came through Windmill a year ago."

"Does it work?" Simon blinked away the tears and stared at the blue sky, green grass, and rolling hills on the other side of the open doorway.

Hard to believe, but it was a working dimensional portal. He'd never seen one outside books. Most people thought they were a myth. Now right before him was evidence they were real.

"Sure. I wouldn't be offering it if it didn't." Wally strode to the window and looked out. "Oh, oh, Mr. Burns brought a couple of Champions goons with him." He shook his head. "I don't think we gotta lot of time." His gaze shifted to Simon. "What do you say, we gotta a deal?"

Simon's eyes narrowed. He smelled a rat. "Where is that?" He nodded to the image on the other side portal.

"Somewhere in the Andromeda galaxy. Or so I'm told."

"So you're told?" It could be a ride to anywhere. That thing could be a simulation interface to fool him.

The perfect escape, right into a trap.

Wally frowned and walked away from the window scratching his bare chest with his nails. "Listen, if you don't want the deal fine by me." He looked at Simon and smiled. "Nice knowing you, boss."

A sharp knock on the door made Simon tense. He had no choice. He had to get off planet now. "The deed to Windmill is in the floor safe under the work bench."

Wally nodded and took another swig from the beer bottle. "Yeah, I know where the safe is, but what's the combination?"

He found the safe? Never in his life had Simon pegged anyone so wrongly as Wally Ogdon. He really had him by the short hairs.

"Jill tells me everything," he added.

It dawned on Simon, Wally added a back door into Jill's program. He knew everything him, everything he'd said to Jill on those lonely nights. The air was suddenly warmer.

"But I told Jill everything." Wally grinned and wiggled his eyebrows suggestively.

Time to give up. "The safes voice activated. The combination is," he paused and his eyes flitted to the scene through the dimensional portal, "you sure about that?"

Wally nodded.

"The combination is alpha-three-seven-alpha."

Wally grunted as he stood as did Simon. "Thanks, boss," he said. The pounding on the door intensified. "I don't think you have any time left."

"Yes." Simon paused and regarded his very clever, very scheming former assistant. "It's been a slice. Take care and thanks again."

Simon's last thought as he stepped through the door way to ask himself why Wally didn't use the portal himself then he was gone.

***

After opening the front door Wally sauntered back to the couch and plunked himself down. Cinder Burns came in, his black orbs focused on the open closet door. The scene through the portal had changed to a rocky beach, crashing surf, and wind bent palm trees.

"Is he gone?" said Burns.

"Yup." Wally tipped back his beer and drained the bottle. After dropping the empty bottle on the couch next to him he emitted a loud burp.

Burns stood before the portal his fists balled on his hips studying the image. "Where did he go?"

Wally shrugged. "How would I know? I wouldn't use the thing. I don't know where anyone goes after they step through."

Burns turned to face him. "Did you get the deed?"

"Sure. I'll have it within the hour. Okay?" Wally avoided looking at the Thom knowing he'd be smiling.

"OK, Mr. Ogdon. That'll be fine." Burns strode to the window and looked out. "The weather here is perfect for us you know."

Wally nodded. "Yeah, I know." He frowned. "Does this settle my debt?"

"Oh, yes more than enough. As you humans are fond of saying; lock, stock, and barrel."

Wally glanced at the Thom standing peering out the window. "I'm leaving in the morning."

The Thom looked at him and nodded. "As I expected." Burns paused then added, "What do you imagine he's doing right now?"

Wally rose off the couch and started walking to the bedroom to dress and begin packing. "Having a beer with Andre I guess," he called before he disappeared down the hallway.

Hook Island

AMANDA HELD OUT THE FLASHLIGHT, but the muddy beam of white light barely penetrated the inky, thick darkness more than a few feet. ahead. Her heart beat loudly in her ears as she carefully stepped forward on the rickety wooden dock. She glanced over her left shoulder to see Pierre in the launch he'd used to bring her to this isolated island off the coast of South Carolina. She swallowed hard and for the hundredth time doubted she'd made the right decision.

"Pierre!" she called. "Which way?"

Squinting into the impenetrable darkness Amanda could just barely make out a man's shape bathed in the glow from the instruments in the dash of the boat.

Pierre was as first understandably reluctant, but once she flashed a hundred dollar bill he readily agreed to transport her to Hook Island. The transplanted Cajun, originally from New Orleans until Hurricane Katrina, was amiable and friendly during the ride from Isle of Palms. She sensed he thought she had a screw loose, but if anyone told her she'd make such a trip in the dead of the night, she might have agreed with him.

"Straight ahead!" she heard his voice echo over the sound of the rhythmic waves ahead of her in the darkness.

Amanda swiveled her head back and forth still unable to see her way along dock. Night vision wasn't her best feature. A strange skill not to have when you're a paranormal investigator since she often worked at night. Her breathing was rapid and her mouth and nose were filled with the smell of wet sand, salt air, and the acidic odor of rotting seaweed. "Too bad I can't lose my sense of smell on command," she mused under her breath.

She carefully moved one foot ahead, the boards creaked. If she didn't walk off the edge of the old dock no doubt it would collapse beneath her.

She should have come in the daytime, but the letter said it was a matter of life and death.

She had seen enough ghosts to know death intimately so she dropped everything back home on Boston and caught the first plane to Charleston. Of course, the certified check for five thousand dollars certainly added to her motivation to come quickly.

Such a large amount of money as a deposit surprised her until she did some research on the plane using her IPad. According to the websites she surfed her mysterious benefactor, Phillip Swann was a descendant of the notorious pirate, Captain Henry "Blackblood" Swann who sailed these waters in the mid 18th century. Captain Swann pillaged French, British, and Spanish ships for valuables, slaves, coffee, and anything else of value. There were suggestions once he captured a ship he set the crew adrift in lifeboats, then set fire to their ships. This last part of the legend was unconfirmed, but if true then Swann wasn't as despicable as many of his contemporaries.

Her problem right now wasn't proving the truth behind the musty legend, it was surviving the trip from the dock to the Swann family house somewhere on this speck of sand and rock. She'd survived worse, but not being able to see where she was going in pitch blackness had always been her greatest fear.

The light from her flashlight flickered twice then went out. Just great, she thought.

Now what I am gonna do?

She stuck the tip of her tongue out one side of her mouth and concentrated on her footing. She then took one step and heard a crack as her foot dropped through a hole in the boards. Oh, oh. Not good.

Trying to extract her foot she lost her balance and stumbled forward. She lost her grip on the small suitcase in her right hand and it flew away from her to be lost somewhere in the darkness. A twinge of relief came over her when she heard it land on sand. At least her extra blue jeans, shorts, and tops would be dry. And her IPad and cell phone would still function. Salt water destroyed electronic gear thoroughly and quickly. Without her equipment her trip to Hook Island would have been pointless. If there was a ghost she would need photographic evidence. No photos, no future book, no future book, no food on table. Girl's gotta eat.

Knowing she was about to fall off the dock she held out her hands, closed her eyes and got ready to break the inevitable as best she could. Hopefully she wouldn't break anything important. She fell forward and found herself sprawled face down on sand. Her mouth had filled with the stuff and she spat out the sticky grains as best she could but the annoying grit was stubborn and wasn't going without a fight. She'd never liked the beach.

There was too much sand, too much wind, and too much salt water for her liking.

When she tried to lift her head overwhelming dizziness gripped her accompanied by a wave of nausea. She set her head back on the sand. The feelings passed but she realized there was a half buried stone in the sand sticking up. She must have struck her forehead against it. A growing warmth pooled around her forehead confirming her theory that she was bleeding. The unmistakable odor of blood flooded her nostrils. Oh, crap. So not good.

She suppressed the urge to cry. I'm going to die on a desert island, in the dark, alone. She investigated the paranormal, she didn't want to be part of it, at least not yet. I'm too young to die.

The panic gripping her faded replaced by rationality. I need to stop wallowing in self pity, she scolded herself. Just because Paul left with the cat doesn't mean I have to fall to pieces during every tiny crisis. Oh, oh...as if a window closed Amanda's world abruptly disappeared.

***

Amanda's eyes fluttered open and through fuzzy vision came streaks of filtered sunlight across a wooden ceiling. Her vision cleared and she shifted her head to her left. There was a window framed by shredded curtains. The glass in the window was missing so a breeze made the curtains move and billow like torn rags in the wind.

Shifting her legs she realized she lay on her back, her head rested on a severely squashed pillow. The air reeked of dust and mildew. Her mouth was devoid of moisture. She ran her tongue over her dry lips then gradually raised up on her elbows until she sat up. She blinked and her dry eyeballs clicked.

Her head throbbed. Instinctively she placed one hand on the side of her head and her fingers brushed a bandage wrapped around her wounded noggin. Now she recalled the fall at the dock. It must have been a while ago since it wasn't night anymore as evidenced by the sunlight creating a spotlight effect on the dirty wood floor.

She froze when from a corner of her left eye she saw movement. Looking down she saw a black cat with a white tipped tail padding across the room on it's paws. Unable to look away Amanda watched the cat until it vanished into the wall.

Her heart beat hard in her chest and she sucked in a breath. The cat hadn't been real, at least not anymore. It was a ghost.

Amanda had seen strange things but never an actual ghost. Most of the paranormal activity she'd witnessed was minor stuff, objects moving by themselves, sudden fluctuations in room temperature, mysterious breezes on a calm night, and things that go bump in the night. She'd never seen a real, live ghost. Uhhhh...correction, a real dead ghost.

Amanda let her head sink back to the pillow and closed her eyes. I must be seeing things...

"Hello, Miss Dark?"

Amanda's eyes popped open and standing at the side of the bed was a square jawed man, his chin and cheeks covered in dark stubble. His jet black curly hair was cut short and his eyes were as blue as a Caribbean sea. His lips formed a wry smile and his eyes twinkled.

"Uhhh...yeah...I'm Amanda Dark." Her brow wrinkled as she eyed the man. "Are you Phillip Swann?"

He nodded. "You really didn't have to come out here in the middle of the night."

She cringed inside. He was correct of course, but for some reason she sensed he needed her as soon as possible. She had no idea where the sense of urgency came from, just that it had.

"You're right, of course, Mr. Swann."

He chuckled. "Mr. Swann was my father. Please call me Phillip." His smile disappeared and he arched one eyebrow sending a shiver of longing through her. She had never had a steady boyfriend since high school, when immediately after the grad party Dave Allister announced he was going back east to college and broke up with her. He broke her heart. That was of course after they'd had sex for the first time.

Since then she'd been on a few dates but nothing stuck. Of course after college she'd become a paranormal investigator. Men didn't seem to like women who chased dead things. When Paul left he made that much clear.

"Hello, Phillip," she held out her right hand which he grasped lightly in his as they shook hands. His warm gentle touch sent shock waves of desire through her unlike anything she'd ever experienced not even with Dave in the back seat of his fathers Durango back in her high school days.

"I thought I'd better come as quickly as possible," she explained. "Your letter said it was a matter of life and death."

Phillip's cheeks glowed crimson, his eyes averted looking at her instead he looked in the direction of the window.

He moved away to the window and gazed out at the rolling surf of the ocean beyond the few trees sticking up from the tan colored sand in front of them.

Amanda rose to a seated position and then swung her legs over the side of the bed. Her head throbbed but she ignored the pain. She came up behind him and detected a sense of sadness emanating from Phillip. For most of her life she'd had a gift of empathy. She couldn't read minds but had a strong sense of their feelings.

It certainly made her life interesting at times, and not always for the good. Back in high school she'd managed to avoid the bullies when she detected their bad feelings toward her. Of course it didn't hurt when your best friend Mary Olson, was captain of the lacrosse team. Mary was as tough as any boy and had been known to flatten a few.

Amanda placed a hand on Phillip's shoulder. He jerked his shoulder away from her touch as if her skin were on fire. "Sorry," she whispered dropping her arm to her side she waited.

He turned to face her. He forced a thin smile on his lips. "I'm sorry, it's just my wife..." His voice trailed off and his next words caught in his throat.

"I'm sorry, I didn't know you're married." She sensed his sadness. "Did she die or something?"

Phillip watery gaze locked with hers. "No. She's alive and living in Alaska. With my ex-partner."

Amanda wondered if maybe she'd tread on forbidden ground. "Sorry. It's none of my business. I —"

"It's okay, Miss Dark. You're empathy is a gift. Yes, I know about your ability to sense feelings. I wondered if it were true when I hired you. I can see it is, maybe a little too true."

Amanda raised both eyebrows. "What do you mean?"

"My wife left me ten years ago. We were high school sweethearts but after that it became clear our lives were on different paths. I still care about Julie, but we've both moved on."

Testing of her abilities was expected so Amanda wasn't insulted or annoyed. Honestly if she was in a client's shoes she would doubt her as well. When you say it out loud a woman who chases ghosts for a living sounds like rubber room time. "Are you married now?" She winced. "Sorry, that's really none of my business."

Phillip laughed. "No worries. I'm just glad you're here." He arched an eyebrow. "And, no I'm not married. Divorced."

Time to change the subject. "Did you see a cat?"

The sexy smile disappeared from Phillip's features. He frowned. "Cat? Was it black with a white tipped tale?" Amanda nodded. "And did it disappear out this window." He pointed to the window. "Or through a wall?"

Amanda's eyes widened. "How did you know?"

Phillip nodded. "Come with me into the old library."

Amanda followed him out of the bedroom into a musty hallway. The walked side by side to the end of the hall where there were double doors. The original brass handles were now black with age lay on the floor where they had fallen as the doors rotted away.

Phillip pushed the doors open with one hand and they went in. The old library walls were covered in shelves of rotting books. The odor of decay was heavy in the air. At one end of room sat a large grandly carved oak desk. On the desk was a hand carved wooden box about the size of modern briefcase. Only it clearly wasn't modern. The carvings depicted slaves harvesting tobacco leaves, and images of a sailing vessel with its sails bulging from the wind. There was also an image of a grinning skull over crossed swords, a classic motif for flags of the pirate age.

Amanda concluded the box had once been the property of one Captain Blackblood Swann, Phillip's ancestor. Her eyes flitted to Phillip then back at the box. Phillip certainly didn't look like a bloodthirsty pirate, and not like any of the ugly pirates in those Disney movies. Actually he looked more the pirates adorning the covers of steamy romance novels. A sun warmed face turned nut brown, dark curls, and muscular arms clearly visible beneath his jean shirt, the top two buttons of which were undone to reveal a wisp of dark hair. His looks alone stirred her more than any man had in a long time.

Phillip moved to the desk and flipped the lid of the box open to reveal a well worn, leather bound book inside. A strong smell of leather filled the room. He gingerly lifted it from the box and set in flat on the desk. Carefully as if handling a baby he turned the yellowed pages to the middle of the thick volume.

Amanda stepped closer to study the odd writing. The words were written in the style of calligraphy, the words ornate and flowing. "What is it?" she asked.

"The diary of Captain Henry Swann."

Amanda's eyes widened. "Really? It must be old."

"Very," he nodded. "The pages are brittle with age so after we find the treasure I plan to donate the book to the Smithsonian."

Treasure? A frown creased Amanda's brow. I nearly kill myself and the life and death mission I'm on is to help him find gold and silver? Amanda wasn't rich, in fact she was on the low side of the middle class, but she wasn't a treasure hunter. To her contact with paranormal phenomena wasn't about seeking lost objects, or obscene wealth, it was to help the dead achieve their just reward or at least be released from earth to go on their way. Sometimes they didn't appreciate her intervention but the living relatives often did.

"What's this about treasure?" she said straining to keep the anger in her gut from her tone.

Phillip swiveled to face her. He offered her a lopsided grin. "Sorry, I'm not a treasure hunter if that's what you're thinking."

Amanda eyed him with one eyebrow cocked. Did he have her ability to sense emotions too? "What does his diary say?"

Phillip's shifted back to gaze down at the pages of the open book. "Captain Swann's diary says he had a cat. A black cat with a white tipped tail. It's name was Scars."

Amanda's eyes went wide and she stepped to his side her eyes on the pages. "Really? I saw a cat like that in my room..." Her cheeks grew warm. "Uhhh, I mean your room...uhhh...I mean the bedroom." Oh, crap he's gonna think I'm an idiot. All she wanted to do right now was crawl into a dark corner and die of embarrassment.

Phillip however didn't seem to notice her sudden discomfort. His eyes were on the pages of the book. "Yes, I expect you saw the ghost of his cat."

Amanda shivered as a sudden coldness enveloped her accompanied by a feeling of dread. She's experienced feeling like these before during investigations in haunted houses, but never with this intensity. Her heart beat hard and time seemed to slow down.

A sharp movement at the edge of her left eye made her turn her head slightly toward the movement. What she saw made her freeze and draw in a ragged breath. Her heart beat rapidly. A man dressed in pirate garb with a long saber dangling from his belt, his dark eyes scowling at her, his white frilly shirt stained with dirt stood eyeing her with one hand resting on the hilt of the sword. His free arm cradled the cat she'd seen earlier, it's white tipped tail flicking to and fro. Could it be a hallucination caused by the blow to the head?

"Uhhh, Phillip, do you see him?"

Phillip looked at her his eyes quizzical. "Who?"

Amanda pointed to where the pirate, with his three cornered wide brimmed hat sporting a black feather, stood silently watching them. Phillip scanned the spot she was pointing and shook his head.

"I don't see anything..." His words trailed off, his face became the color of ash. "A ghost," he whispered. His hands were trembling. "You see a ghost don't you?"

"Yes. At least I think I do."

"You mean you've never seen one before?"

Amanda swallowed hard as she placed one hand on his arm. She needed to steady herself before she collapsed. Her heart pounded hard in her chest and her armpits leaked like Niagara falls. Any second her knees would buckle and she'd give a sack of potatoes competition to the floor. "As strange as it sounds, no, I've never seen a live one....uhhh, I mean a dead one..." Her mouth clamped shut to stop herself before she shoved both feet into it.

"What's he look like?"

Amanda shifted her gaze to the pirate who eyed her curiously. He carried the cat to a chair across the room, sat down now petting the cat with his other hand. The cat curled it's tail lazily around it's body and looked very content.

It's unblinking mustard yellow eyes watched her.

"Well, he's a pirate and he has a cat. He's sitting on the chair —"

"Sorry to interrupt, Amanda, but there aren't any chairs in here. Haven't been in about two hundred years."

"Actually, the pirate's sitting on one right over there..." Amanda nodded to the spot where the pirate sat watching her. He wore a half smile on his lips now. Amanda's fear had dissipated, replaced by growing annoyance. He was laughing at her. She was the only one who could see him and he finds her predicament funny. Truthfully she'd find her hard to believe too.

"Listen, Phillip, if I tell you there's a pirate over there sitting on a chair then there is. I never lie. I don't know why I see him, or his cat, and he may be the first ghost I've seen in the fles — in person, but I am a paranormal investigator. It's my job. It's what I do." She wasn't sure the pirate was real but she wasn't about to let anyone think badly of her chosen profession. Too many people thought paranormal investigators were scam artists and charlatans. Until they needed her services.

Phillip held up his hands in mock surrender.

"Ok, ok, I did check you out. I know you're a paranormal investigator and according to my sources you're a darned good one."

Amanda took a step away from him and eyed him with a scowl marring her forehead. "You checked me out. With whom?"

Phillip dropped his arms to his sides, rolled his eyes, and emitted a soft chuckle. "Trust me, Amanda it's nothing untoward I assure you. I'm a lawyer in Boston, where you also live, and I have a client who used your unique services a couple of years back. Do you remember Ollie Hardson?"

She did indeed remember Ollie, the man she dubbed the roamer because his hands often ended up in the wrong places like on her bottom at the most inappropriate times. She also recalled helping him remove the ghost of his dead Aunt Grace from his ancestral home. Of course, he then sold the old house to a developer for a small fortune. It's a strip mall now.

"You know, Ollie?" she said.

Phillip snorted. "Yeah. Real creep." He shook his head. "I did the legal work on the sale of house you cleared of his aunt's ghost. He told me all about it." He chuckled.

"Never seen a guy so scared in all my life. His story reminded me of the ghost stories we used to tell around the fire at camp Woebegone when I was a kid. But if there was one thing about Ollie he convinced me the tale wasn't fantasy."

Maybe Phillip wasn't such a bad guy. If he was telling the truth. "Why don't you tell me what this is really all about?"

Phillip glanced at the watch on his left wrist. "I imagine you're hungry. Why don't we eat and I'll tell you all about it? And then if you don't want to help me fine, you can keep the money and I'll call for a boat to take you back to Iles of Palms, no questions asked. Deal?"

Amanda considered his words. Phillip Swann was growing on her. And he seemed trustworthy, for a lawyer. She nodded. "Deal." Her stomach rumbled. She looked at Phillip her eyes wide with horror. He laughed first, then she joined in.

Before they left the library Amanda stole a quick glance at Captain Swann still seated with the Scars curled in his lap. He nodded when she walked passed him. His expression was pleasant. A pleasant pirate, who woulda thought?

***

Phillip surprised her when they went out the back door off the kitchen of the old house. The kitchen was beyond repair, every wooden surface was cracked by wind and heat, the glass in the window frames here too were absent so there was nothing to keep out the inclement weather when winter storms brushed the island. Phillip explained the family home had been abandoned just prior to the civil war. Parts of the house were damaged when the Confederate army used the house as a headquarters form which to launch troops or ships against Union forces. In an attempt to drive out the rebel army the Union navy bombarded the island just as they had nearby Fort Sumter, but never succeeded in dislodging the Confederate troops.

At the rear of the house, Phillip had erected a tent, and to create his own shaded area he'd tied the corners of a tarp to the trees ringing his campsite. In the center of the camp was a fire pit, a shallow pit dug in the soft sand and clay, a ring of large smoke blackened rocks with a stainless steel grate covered the pit. Off a tripod over the pit hung a steel hook with an old-fashioned cast iron cooking pot.

"Water?" Phillip asked waving her to a camp chair to the right of the fire pit. She nodded and sat in the chair. The air was rife with wood smoke. To the left of the tent was a pile of firewood.

He went to an orange cooler and took out two bottles of water one of which he handed to her before squatting next to the pit and lighting the fire. Soon a blue and yellow flame danced under the grate the wood snapping and popping as the moisture in the wood was heated and expelled. A trial of white smoke disappeared into the sky over head.

Amanda broke the seal on the bottle and twisted off the cap. After taking a long swig of the cool water she put the cap back on the bottle and placed it in her lap. "You seem to have been here for a while."

Phillip was busy concentrating on nursing the growing fire. "Yeah," he said, "a while. I was waiting for you. I sent the letter two weeks ago." He shrugged. "I didn't know how long it would take so I may have over prepared."

The fire crackled brightly and the flames now licked the grate. Satisfied Phillip rose to his feet and moved to cooler again. "Hotdogs okay?" Since tubes of mystery meat were one of her favorite food groups, Amanda readily agreed, but just as she did at home promised herself to eat better in future.

He glanced at her and grinned. "Good. Mustard, ketchup?" Again she nodded.

Soon they were eating barbecue hotdogs in silence, the smoke from the fire permeating everything.

Amanda swallowed a bite of meat, bun, and the mustard-ketchup mixture. She broke the silence first. "What's in the treasure that you're so interested in if it's not gold and jewels?"

Phillip stopped eating and looked at her. His eyes were serious, she worried she may have offended him. "I'm hoping the chest buried somewhere on this island holds the truth about my famous ancestor."

Her curiosity aroused Amanda continued. "I gather there is a letter or document that will tell a different story about Captain Swann than the tales told in the history books?"

Phillip took a small bite of his hotdog and nodded. "Yes. I believe there is a letter signed by the Queen Anne of England affirming Captain Swann was an agent of the Queen in the Caribbean, raiding Spanish and French colonies and their ships to disrupt trade."

"That's very different than what's recorded about your ancestor." Amanda frowned. "Why does this matter so much to you now? Surely after three hundred years it doesn't really matter all that much does it?"

Phillip's face became a mask of determination, his jaw line taunt. He threw the remainder of his meal into the fire. The fatty meat flared and she could smell it charring. "Before my father died of cancer last year he made me promise to clear the Swann name." He stopped and looked into her eyes. She saw his eyes lose their hard edge and his shoulders relaxed. "Sorry. I must seem a little obsessed. I may be, but Dad always felt the reason Captain Swann's name was dishonored involved family land claims in England."

Amanda curled an eyebrow. "Land claims?"

"Yes. When Queen Anne died in 1714 King Charles I assumed the throne. He was German and had little interest in English affairs of state, those he left to Sir Robert Walpole. The Walpole's and the Swann's were not on the best of terms since the Walpole's wanted the Swann lands, and because of a love affair that ended badly between cousins from each family."

Sounds like Romeo and Juliet, thought Amanda. She took a bite of her hotdog, chewed and swallowed. "They didn't like each other, so what does this all have to do with Queen Anne's letter?"

Phillip shook his head. "Walpole had all copies of the letter destroyed and announced that the English navy would hunt down Captain Swann and hang him as a pirate, which they did in 1719.

"What Walpole didn't know was a single copy of Queen Anne's letter with the royal seal remained hidden on this island. Over the years we've tried many times to find it without success."

Amanda finished her meal and felt rejuvenated. She took a sip of water then said, "You want me to ask Captain Swann where the chest is hidden. Correct?"

"Yes."

"And I suppose there are jewels and gold buried with the document."

Phillip smiled. "I don't know. And frankly I don't care."

"But I do," said a deep male voice to Amanda's left. Looking to the row of trees where the voice came from she saw a tall, dark skinned man step out from behind a tree. Her heart froze. In his right hand he held a snub nosed pistol pointed at them.

Phillip chuckled. "Ahhh, yes, Jim Sweet, my former partner. How nice of you to drop by. How long have you been listening?"

The corner of Sweet's mouth curled up. "Long enough to know you may have found the key to finding the treasure." He waved the gun at Amanda. "Her."

Phillip made a move to stand, but Sweet waved the pistol at him. "Don't move," Sweet said his eyes narrowing.

Phillip shoulders slumped and he remained seated. "OK, Jim, you win. What do you want?"

"I want this little lady to accompany me inside the house, talk the ghost into telling me where the treasure is hidden, and then I'll be on my way."

Phillip arched an eyebrow. "What about me?"

"I was thinking I'd dispose of you first, but if the captain won't talk to me I may still need you. So I'm going to tie you up and leave you here. If I need you I'll come back for you, if not..." Jim left the rest to their imagination, not that it needed much imagination to see he was going to kill them both regardless of what happened. As the pirates used to say, dead men tell no tales.

If there was a treasure buried with the letter about Captain Swann it would be worth a fortune in today's money. People have killed for far less.

"You," Sweet pointed the pistol at her, "find a rope and tie him up."

Amanda looked to Phillip. He nodded and pointed to the tent. "There's a rope inside."

Amanda's face grew cold. They were going along with this man? Why?

Soon, after some instruction by Sweet, she had Phillip tied to the chair and his mouth stuffed with a piece of dirt stained cloth.

"Let's go," Sweet said his voice menacing, his eyes flat with no emotion. How did Phillip get hooked up with such a man, someone capable of killing in cold blood.

Amanda started walking toward the house followed by Sweet who had the gun pressed into her back. One thing her father insisted she learn before she left home to move to the big city was how to use and care for guns. She didn't really like guns, but when someone has one pressed into your spine, knowledge could in handy. Six hours a week at a gun range for three months made a girl fairly proficient with firearms.

She entered the house and went immediately to the library where they'd left the diary open on the weathered desk. Amanda was disappointed to see the chair and Captain Swann with his cat were missing.

Moving to the book she pretended to be read it. Her eyes flitted to movement as Sweet came from behind to stand beside her. He had the gun pointing to the floor at his side. He didn't see her as a threat.

A small smile played across Amanda's lips. Once his attention was on the book she decided her opportunity would never be better so she reached for the gun and managed to grab it and twist it out of his hand before he could react.

Stepping away she raised the weapon and pointed it at Sweet's chest. A quick glance confirmed the safety was off.

Sweet regarded her with his dead eyes. "Go ahead," he said, "shoot." He took a step toward her and she instinctively took a step back.

One thing her father hadn't taught her was the killer instinct. Shooting paper targets was very different from shooting a living person. Her fingers gripping the pistol began to sweat. "Don't move," she said.

"I don't think you'll fire," said Sweet stepping closer. He raised one hand and slowly reached for the gun.

"Don't! I will you know..."

Sweet grabbed the barrel of the pistol and pulled it from her slick fingers. Amanda's heart sank. She'd failed them both. They were going to die.

Sweet smiled grimly. "Now stop this nonsense and talk to the ghost about the treasure." He pointed the gun at her forehead. "Right now." he growled, "Or I will shoot you, and I won't chicken out."

"Sweet!" It was Phillip's voice. Suddenly Sweet and the pistol were gone. At her feet lay the tangled mass of two men locked in combat.

Amanda backed up until her body was pressed against the wall, while watching the struggling men.

Phillip landed a punch on Sweet's jaw,, his head snapped to the right. Bones crunched and she could see Philips knuckles were inflamed. Sweet grunted from the blow and his head snapped back. He raised the pistol, which miraculously he hadn't let go of when Phillip tackled him.

Gritting his teeth Phillip grabbed Sweets arm, twisted it hard backward causing the pistol to fly out of his hand. The gun struck the wall behind them with a thud, then rattled to the floor. Amanda considered going for the weapon, but if she tried she might be knocked to the floor by the two men fighting. The room was too small for her to maneuver around them. They leaped to their feet and circled each other warily. Sweet's eyes kept flicking from Phillip to the gun then back again. Phillip's attention was focused solely on his opponent.

Sweet hands formed fists. He leapt forward and swung a fist hard at Phillip's head. Phillip ducked inside Sweet's intended blow and landed a hard blow to Sweet's solar plexus.

The air rushed from Sweet's lungs, he gasped clutching his belly as he stumbled backward. Phillip stepped forward, landed a punch hard on Sweet's chin. The man's head snapped around and he collapsed into a heap on the floor where he lay still, his eyes closed.

It was over. Phillip had won.

He moved unsteadily on rubbery legs, his lip was bleeding. His left cheek sported a purple bruise that was already badly swollen. He dragged air into his lungs.

Amanda rushed to him. She wrapped her arms around him, partially to keep him from falling and partially to comfort him. She grasped him by his shoulders and studied his bloodshot eyes. "Phillip, thank you for saving me."

He gave her a weak smile. "No worries."

"Who is he?" She nodded toward Sweet laying unconscious on the floor.

"My former law partner," Phillip said.

Amanda's eyes went wide. "He's a lawyer? Would he have really killed us?"

"Oh, yes. He was convicted of murdering his wife, and his mother-in-law. And that was for one hundred thousand dollars in insurance money. A priceless treasure proved too much for a greedy creep like him." His eyes drooped at the corners. "I should never have told him about my ancestor, but I thought he was my friend."

A cold dread washed over her sending chills up her spine. Maybe it was emanating from Sweet or Phillip, but she didn't think so.

After releasing Phillip he leaned in to the wall and watched her as she moved to the desk and opened the diary again. She looked back to the spot where she'd seen the pirate before, sure enough there he was seated as before on the chair with the cat in his lap.

"Hello, lass," he said. There was definitely an English inflection in his voice.

Amanda thought for a second or two she might faint. Not only had she seen her first ghost, but he'd just spoken to her.

"Uhhh...hello?"

Phillip frowned. "Who are you talking to?"

"He's here again."

"Oh. Quick before he leaves again, ask him where the treasure is hidden."

Amanda opened her mouth to speak, but the ghost rose from the chair his hand resting on the hilt of his sword, the cat dropped to all fours it's tail wagging. "Why should I?" he said.

"Is something wrong?" asked Phillip.

This go-between conversation could get complicated. She had to discover another way to get these two together. "Captain. I'm wondering if you will show yourself to Phillip." She indicated Phillip with a slight nod of her head. The ghost scowled. He didn't appear open to the idea.

Perhaps if she shared some information about him the captain might be more agreeable.

"Captain. I'd like to introduce you to your great-great-great grandson, Phillip Swann. The ghost arched one eyebrow. She'd tweaked his interest, but not secured his cooperation. Time to go for broke. She wondered if ghosts had traces of their human emotions remaining. She hoped so if not than this would fall flatter than the Soufflé she tried to make once in Home Ed class. "Before his father died he asked Phillip to clear his family name."

The ghosts eyebrows rose together and his dark eyes narrowed. "What trickery be this, lass? I am charged by the Queen herself to be her agent in these waters."

"That was three hundred years ago. You were betrayed by Lord Walpole who branded you as a pirate and had you hung in 1719." The ghost of Captain Swann ran one hand across his throat. She knew she'd triggered a buried memory, and not a pleasant one. She continued her explanation. "Lord Walpole had all copies of the letter destroyed expect the one you hid here on the island. In order to clear your name in the history books, we need that letter."

Captain Swann frowned then said, "OK, lass, the boy can see me now."

Amanda's eyes flicked to Phillip. His face was pale and his eyes wide. He indeed could see the pirate captain. She worried it might be too much for him especially in his weakened condition. As she watched his features relaxed and his demeanor changed. His face became calm and his eyes reflected determination. "Captain Swann. Sir. I'm your great-great-great grandson, Phillip — "

The ghost captain interrupted him with a burst of laughter his features were now split by a wide grin. "Weren't ya listen to the lass here, boyo. She told me yor tale of woe. Or should ah say my tale of woe."

Phillip's eyes flitted to Amanda and his cheeks flushed crimson. "Yes, of course." He smiled weakly at her. "She's a special lady with special powers."

"Lad, if ya press the palm of yor hand six inches to the right of the corner where the two walls meet a hidden panel will open. Inside ya'll find the letter from mah Queen." With those words the captain faded then disappeared. Looking around Amanda saw Scars the cat had also disappeared.

"Wow. That was something," said Phillip expelling the breath he'd been holding in. "Do you still see him?" he said looking at Amanda. She shook her head.

"Let's see what's hidden in the wall," she suggested.

Phillip moved to the corner and pressed the wall as the ghost instructed. There was a soft click then as if it were on a hinge a portion of the wall from the floor to the ceiling swung inward. The section was no more than six inches wide, not enough to hide a treasure chest that much was clear. Dust accompanied the panel opening. Amanda sneezed when the dust filled her nose.

"Bless you," said Phillip. He reached into the open panel and pulled out a four foot long tube-shaped leather case. It had a carrying strap on one side and the size and shape suggested it might contain a map.

Amanda's heart beat rapidly, she was anxious to see what was inside. Phillip carried it to the desk she followed. They stood side by side as he opened the top of the case and peered inside. A smile played across his lips which became a full blown grin.

"I see a document inside."

"Is it a map?"

"Yes, tell us, Phil is there a treasure map in there?"

Amanda froze and shut her eyes tight. Oh, crap, Sweet's awake. A soft click told her he had the pistol. They were right back where they started. Doomed.

"Well, well ya, scurvy dog, do ya think I'd let the likes o' you get the drop on me family?"

A bloodcurdling scream made the hair on the back of her neck stand at attention and sent shivers down her spine. The scream ended abruptly as if a tap had been turned off. Amanda opened one eye to steal a look at Phillip. He too had his eyes shut.

After several seconds of silence that seemed like an eternity Amanda decided to take a look. She opened her eyes and turned around.

There was no sign of Sweet, the captain, or his cat. All that remained was the pistol laying on the floor resting near the wall where their would be murderer must have dropped it. She tapped Phillip on his shoulder, he turned around.

"What happened?" he said.

Amanda shook her head slowly. "I have no idea. I've never known ghosts to interact with the living. Unless..." It couldn't be but it was the only sane explanation, if you could call the paranormal sane. She set her jaw and explained. "I've read about this, but have never met anyone who's seen it. And least anyone who's still alive."

Phillip looked at her in awe his eyes wide. She continued.

"In 1891 a man named Simon Polson, a medium reputed to have been to the other side, reported that when ghosts feel threatened or when they're angered they can will themselves to touch and interact physically with the real world. Polson said it drained them and in some cases destroyed them, but if the ghost were powerful enough they could even drag the living into the spirit world. The living would not be able to escape and would spend eternity neither living nor dead, in limbo."

Phillip shuddered. "Sounds horrible. Do you think that's what happened to Jim?"

Amanda nodded. "Yes, I think so. But as my mother used to say, he made his bed he has to lie in it."

She turned to the desk and picked up the map case. "If this is the letter then we need to take it to a museum to get it authenticated. Old documents will crumble unless they're treated with great care. Do you agree?"

"Yes, but I'm anxious to see the letter."

Amanda grinned. "Me as well, but we have to be patient."

Phillip offered her a lopsided grin which got her juices flowing again. "Perhaps you and I can work together once we get back to Boston. What do you think?"

Amanda wanted to see him again in the worst way possible. Or was it the best? She smiled to herself. "Well, Mr. Swann, since you saved my life I think we can arrange something, but I must insist you let me buy you dinner."

"Agreed." He held out his hand, she took it in hers and shook to seal their agreement. Reluctantly she let go.

"Let's pack up your camp and call for a boat. I'm sure Pierre wouldn't mind coming back for us," she said. Phillip nodded then took the leather case from her and walked out of the library into the hall.

A small movement to her left shifted her attention away from the doorway toward the wall. Scars appeared from the wall padded to her and rubbed his body against her legs emitting a gentle purring sound. She sighed. Not only did she have a new friend and business partner, but somehow she had adopted a ghost cat.

Amanda watched Phillip go and it dawned on her her life was headed on a new path. She might even have discovered a best friend and maybe more, hopefully much more.

Cave of Wonders

SACK'S CRIES OF TERROR AND SOBS of fear sent shock waves through me. Sack pleaded with me to save him. But I my strength was waning and my arms ached from his one hundred fifty pounds pulling at me.

I'm slipping! Panic gripped me.

His weight began to drag me across the wet leaves on my belly toward our mutual assured destruction.

Sack's cries and screams of terror echoed off the tall still forest surrounding us. Except for me there was no one to hear us. Even the bird's had suddenly gone silent. I knew we were both going to fall into the mysterious pit. And nothing on Earth would save us.

Tree rot, damp earth, and a putrid stink my twelve-year-old brain could only describe at the time as death, poured from the sinkhole to fill my nose and mouth with its putrid stench.

We had not seen the sinkhole on the forest floor as we trudged through the Wisconsin maples headed for an ancient cave hidden somewhere along Rattlesnake Creek. Grandma Huffnagle assured us we would find it there. Like every twelve-year-old boy my imagination was fired by the idea of buried treasure, and secret places no other human being had ever seen.

Hubert J. Sacker, I called him Sad Sack or just Sack (after our favorite Saturday paper cartoon strip), and I set off from Beetown early this morning on the Grant county bus. We headed for a deserted stretch of Grassmaker Road near Rattlesnake Creek.

Our plan was to hike in from the road, our pockets full of chocolate bars, in case we got hungry, to find the Cave of Wonders. It was a perfect plan — a foolproof plan —that had suddenly gone awry.

My breathing labored, and my mouth dry, I desperately struggled to keep my best friends from falling. He being twenty pounds heavier than my slender frame made my task all that more difficult.

I slipped some rain slicked leaves as we edged closer to edge of the precipice. My belly scrapped through moist earth accompanied by an orchestra of crunching fall leaves. My friend dangled over the edge of the pit.

Sack began to cry. "I don' wanna die, Huff!" His words echoed from within the bowels of the black pit.

I knew I was going to either have to let go of my best friend and let him fall, or join him and take our chances. I only hoped one of us wasn't so badly hurt after the fall we couldn't climb back to safety, or at least get help for the other.

That is if Grandma's right and we found our way out of the cave at all.

I suddenly shot toward the pit. Red, gold, and yellow leaves flew about me like dried up raindrops then, with out warning, I was thrust over the edge into the dank, dark air.

It seemed like we were the Coyote chasing the roadrunner as we hung in mid-air, Sack's hand still firmly gripped in mine. Then we fell.

The damp air swallowed our screams of terror as we disappeared into the darkness.

***

I don't know how long we were unconscious, but when I opened my eyes I stared into a black void. I recall thinking; Is this what it's like to be dead?

"Huff?" said a small voice I knew to be Sack's followed by a soft groan.

"You alright?" I gasped between gritted teeth.

I tested my fingers and toes by wiggling them and then, after confirming nothing was broken, moved my arms and legs. I seemed to be whole and very much alive. My forehead head felt wet and I had a slight twinge of pain when I tested it with my fingers tips. My fingers came away with something sticky and wet on them. I realized I was bleeding but I had no idea the extent of the wound.

My mouth felt as if it was dried with cotton balls. I ran my tongue over parched lips. I sat up and placed both hands flat on the cave floor. We were lying on a bed of wet leaves that must've cushioned our fall. Lucky.

"Yeah," said Sack. "I think I'm ok…"

He sounded a little dazed so I reached out in the darkness and managed to feel the fabric of his wool jacket. Like me he was sitting up. I patted his arm hoping to reassure him.

Since he looked to me as the leader of our heroic twosome, I knew it was my responsibility to get us out of this jam. "It's ok, pal. I'll get us outta here."

"You still got those chocolate bars?" I felt my jacket pockets and mine were still there.

"Yeah," said Sack.

"Let's eat one and then see if we can find a way outta here."

I pulled out a candy bar, tore off the wrapper and bit into the too sweet milk chocolate. I heard Sack do the same.

We sat in the awful silence the only sound of chewing and swallowing. At least the taste and odor of the sweet chocolate masked the putrid smell of the rotting leaves and something else. Something I didn't want to think about. Buried treasure usually meant dead pirates. Maybe…? I shivered involuntarily.

What bothered me more than anything right now was my bum felt like it was soaked through. God, how I hate a wet butt.

As we ate I found my eyes were beginning to adjust to the gloom around me. I noticed that above us was the sinkhole opening dotted with stars. I recalled feeling an odd sense of reassurance at knowing where we'd come from. Problem was it looked so far away. It was unlikely we would be able to climb out that way so we would need to find another exit.

I squinted hard to see the immediate vicinity around us and managed to spot, across from where we sat, an opening that must lead deeper into the cave. It seemed to me this was our only option. But where were the torches left behind by the pirates?

There were always torches in the movies.

"Can you see me?" I said.

"Sorta," said Sack. He'd always had better night vision that I did. I knew this because one night we were on old man Bloomers farm stealing apples from his tree, when Sack spotted the old man with his shotgun sneaking up on us. Not that Mr. Bloomer would've shot, us but he would certainly have scared us if we hadn't high tailed it outta there, thanks to Sack.

"Can you stand?" I said. I tried to stand. I made it to my feet. I almost fell over from a sudden wave of dizziness that swept over me, but managed to stay on my feet. I stood still and closed my eyes until the queasiness in my stomach subsided. My head throbbed like a toothache. The head wound must be worse than I'd initially thought.

I heard the crunch of leaves. When I opened my eyes, I saw a vague outline that had to be Sack standing beside me.

"You okay?" he said. His voice sounded worried.

"No. Not really." I felt an arm come across my shoulders and then the warmth of Sack's larger frame holding me. "Lean on me," he said sounding suddenly very mature.

I was in no position to argue so I leaned against him then we started to walk.

His long arm supported me as we hobbled toward the opening that looked slightly darker than where we were now. Inky blackness surrounded us requiring us to go slow.

The crunch of leaves disappeared as we approached the shadowy opening. I squinted into the darkness ahead and saw a scattering of white light as if from a reflective pond at night. The light looked very far away but it thrilled me a sense of renewed hope.

"Hey! Look!" said Sack, his voice excited like the day on his tenth birthday when his dad gave him his Daisy carbine. He loved that gun even if it wasn't a real gun. We'd spent many an hour in the woods out back of our houses pretending we were stalking big game in darkest Africa.

With each step toward the light, it became more dazzling like a new summer dawn. Finally, we came to a long tunnel, one wall of which didn't look like dirt or stone. It was composed of slick black stone, smooth and polished to a brilliant shine, like Grandpa's church shoes.

Etched into the stone were human-shaped figures carved in white outline, and animals I didn't recognize.

The figures depicted what looked like men with bows, arrows, and spears attacking animals — a lot of animals. But the animals didn't look normal, at least for Wisconsin in 1966. The animals were larger than anything I'd ever seen around here.

Enormous antlers adorned the head of a massive deer like creature, and one animal even looked like an elephant with a shaggy Beatle cut.

I recalled seeing artist's concepts of such creatures in National Geographic and realized what we were looking at were prehistoric drawings of a hunt.

"Wow!" breathed Sack. "The wall's glowing…"

He was right the light coming from the etchings lit up the chamber. I closed my eyes for a second and then opened them to see the glowing etchings still there. Could the bump on my head be that bad that I'm seeing things? Maybe it was a mirage. I mean, it couldn't be real. But then how did Sack see the same thing I did?

I spotted an adjacent tunnel leading off the chamber. The walls of that tunnel were black as a moonless night. That was until we walked toward the newly discovered tunnel. A large section of the walls suddenly lit up with white light, forcing us to shield our eyes with our arms.

With eyes closed tight, and hands out like Frankenstein, Sack and I willed our feet forward one cautious step at a time. I dropped my arms and squinted into the light until the spots before my eyes diminished and once again I could see where we were headed.

As we came to the lit section it abruptly went dark and another section lit up farther down the tunnel. The lit sections reminded me of the sign above the Bijou in Lancaster. The unlit sections looked like plain old brown dirt. Weird.

It occurred to me later someone or something wanted us to follow them. At the time though, Sack and I exchanged worried glances then shrugged in unison. What choice did we have? It had to be better to keep moving than try to go back into that awful stench in the pit.

At least in here the air, though oddly cool, was a little warmer and contained a fragrance like a blend of washed river stone and rose water. Kinda strange when you think about it, but if this was the cave of wonders, which clearly it was, then everything was going to get stranger still. I recall wishing Grandma Huffnagle had warned us —

A breeze! I felt an involuntary shiver run down my spine and the hair on the back of my neck stood erect. What a rush!

This had to be the way out. I wanted to run for the safety of the world outside, but I was woozy and my legs felt as if they were made of rubber. Sack held me tighter as we came to a place in the tunnel where we could see an entrance to the cave. Visible through the cave mouth were trees and puffy white clouds rolling gently across an azure sky. A sense of relief washed over me.

As we stepped outside, I took in a deep breath of sweet sap, moss and other smells of the living forest. The warm sunshine hitting my face felt good. It felt especially good after being in the damp cave. A shiver ran through my body. The cave had reeked of death and I didn't want to ever go in there again.

We'd be home soon. We hadn't found pirate treasure but we'd certainly had an adventure. I for one had had my fill of adventure for a lifetime.

Now to the first order of business: I knew my head wound needed immediate attention. Where's the road?

I looked around and didn't see anything familiar. We must've been in the cave for a long time. Far longer than it seemed, because when we'd fallen in it was mid- afternoon. Now the sky now looked as if it were early morning.

And the forest floor appeared undisturbed, strewn as it was with pale dusky earth and moss covered rocks and bits of twig and bark shed by the gray and white birch trees that grew amongst the maples.

"Do you see the way we came —" I started to say when something odd struck me. "Sack. I don't think we're in Kansas anymore…"

He laughed. I felt his large frame shudder against me. "Don' be silly, Huff. We're in Wisconsin."

I shook my head then turned to gaze into his green eyes. "That's not what I mean. Look at the trees."

A puzzled frown crossed Sack's features then a look of concentration as he scanned the forest of maple and birch trees that surrounded us swaying in unison to a tune only they could hear.

"I don't see —" Sack's mouth became a thin line and his normally rosy cheeks paled. His eyes popped wide.

"Huh…I don' git it…how did the leaves get back on them trees?"

***

When we finally we found the road it looked ancient and unused.

Two worn wagon ruts dug deep into the dark soil of the forest floor, and a strip of long, scraggy grass sliced the middle of the twin depressions.

Some of the longer blades had bloomed at the ends and were faded by the summer sun to the color of pale wheat.

All around us, birds called to each other from treetops. Their songs were accompanied by the clicks of crickets and frogs, speaking in some alien tongue no human would ever understand. It was as if we were surrounded by a chorus of nature.

Though I knew it was a lost cause, we decided to follow the rough road in the hopes that it would lead us to civilization and help. Already darkness edged my vision and I knew if we didn't find someone soon I was going to fall into a sleep from which I'd most certainly never awake.

We plodded along slowly, me forcing one foot in front of the other, and Sack's mood becoming more frantic with each step, until we saw a girl about our age walking in the ruts toward us.

Her red-orange hair, and a pale face dotted with freckles, made her stand out against the green forest on either side of the road. She was dressed in faded blue coveralls, and a matching work shirt that rose above the neckline of the coveralls.

On her feet were black leather shoes that were scuffed and worn.

Her head was down when we first saw her and she was swinging a stick back and forth across the strip of grass, softly singing a tune quickly lost to us in the breeze.

When Sack spotted her, he shouted to get her attention. She paused in her wandering, her eyes coming up and stared wide-eyed at us. Her eyes were as green as the pale sea green earrings my mom wore on special occasions.

A frown crossed her features, as if she were considering something, then she began to run toward us, tossing her stick to the side of the road in the short brush that abutted the trees on either side. Her shoes kicked up a cloud of pale dust as she ran, her cool gaze fixated on me until she stood in front of us.

"You OK?" she said, her voice high pitched but not annoying, like our fifth grade teacher, Miss Arnold.

I smiled weakly and shook my head.

"What do ya think?" said Sack, a trace of annoyance in his voice. He'd never had much patience for girls. Something his Mom said he'd out grow in a few years, but I doubted he would ever change.

"Com'on," she said motioning for us to follow her off the road into the forest.

"There's nothin' that way," said Sack.

The girl smiled warmly and her eyes sparkled with unabashed amusement. "Trust me," she said then turned and began to walk toward the stand of maples and birches.

Something about the way she said it made a warm feeling come over me. Maybe it was the hit on the head, but there was something very familiar in her voice.

"It's okay. Let's follow," I said. Sack shrugged and we began to follow her.

Soon we were in amongst the woods feeling as if we'd never left them. Within a few minutes that seemed like hours, we entered a clearing.

In the center of the clearing was a small house with, a trail of gray smoke coming from a black metal chimney sticking from wood shingles on the roof. I'd never seen anything like it, this side of the fairy tale cottages I'd seen in picture books when I was five.

"Mother!" said the girl suddenly, startling me.

A woman with dark hair, tied in a bun on top of her head, came out of the front door of the house, her shoes creaking on the wooden slats that made up the porch. She wore a plain brown floor-length dress and a gray-white long sleeved shirt. A plain dirt brown apron covered the front of the dress.

With one hand, she pushed a few stray hairs off her face as she gazed in our direction.

Her eyes went wide as she saw us trailing behind our new red-haired friend. She hurried toward us with one hand holding her dress off the forest floor.

Stopping in front of us, she looked me over as if I were a newborn baby, and then to my surprise she wrapped one hand around my left side. Sack was already supporting my right side, so together they carried me toward the house.

At this point, I didn't care if these people were kidnappers, white slavers, or pirates. All I knew for sure is I needed help.

"My lord, boy, what happened to you?" she said, her voice was deep but feminine at the same time.

"I fell into a cave," I said weakly.

"Cave? There's no caves 'round here," she said. "But never mind right now. Let's get you inside and get that wound tended to. You look to me like you've lost a lot of blood." She glanced at the girl who was obviously her daughter. "Ada, you fetch my medicines and meet me by the fire."

"Yes ma'am," said the girl, who then disappeared toward a small wooden shed that stood to the left of the house.

Once inside I saw much the walls, like the outside of the structure, were comprised of rough untreated wood. The floor was made of wooden planks, not like the polished hardwood at my Dad's brother's house, but real wooden planks, rough and unfinished that creaked loudly as we walked across them.

Cooking odors came from a black cauldron suspended over a crackling fire in a stone fireplace. The room was filled with the smells of chicken, vegetables, and potatoes causing my stomach to emit a low growl, that I hoped no one could hear but me.

The woman looked at me and smiled warmly. "Well, well," she said, "you can't be that bad. Your stomach is certainly sending us signals isn't it?"

I suppressed a laugh knowing it would make my head ache and managed a weak smile instead. My face felt warm and I knew I must be red as my Dad's pickup.

Once near the fire she sat me down in a worn, cloth-covered wing chair. I collapsed like some drunken sailor returning from a Saturday night pass. Not that I knew what being drunk was like at the time, but I'd seen drunks in movies.

The girl reappeared at her mother's side with a black, leather-wrapped bundle, tied together with rough twine.

Sack stepped back and watched me, a worried expression on his features. I nodded at him and mouthed that everything would be okay.

The woman took the bundle from her daughter and smiled lovingly at her. She then knelt beside me placing the bundle next to her on the fireplace hearth.

She undid the twine and I saw there were dried plants in the bundle, each wrapped separately as if they were a surgeons tools. She reached for one brown dried bundle and gently, as if she were handling fine crystal, undid the string around it.

The woman picked one long piece of dried plant pressed it onto my forehead and closed her eyes. She began to speak in a language I didn't recognize. Not that I knew any beyond what I'd learned in school, but it certainly didn't sound like anything I'd ever heard. Even to this day, I don't know what language she spoke.

Instantly I felt the pain in my head subside and strength begin to flow back into my body. It was as if I was being filled with energy. What's happening to me?

Soon I felt as if I'd slept for twelve hours. The woman eased back onto her haunches and sighed heavily her eyes still closed. Now she looked as if she could use some rest. Odd. She looked older than before my treatment. How is that possible?

Opening her eyes she said, "I'm going to lie down, Ada. You stay here with the boys." With those words she stood and disappeared through a door leading off the main room.

Not that there was much to the room. It had a few wood chairs that were also roughed wood with no evidence of paint or varnish having ever touched any surface.

What was obviously a cooking area contained no refrigerator or stove. I recall thinking it very odd they had no modern appliances, but decided these people were probably hippies from San Francisco. Or maybe aliens as silly at that sounds now in hindsight.

There were shelves lining one wall with wooden bowls and tin plates resting in short stacks on them. And not very many at that.

Finally, I decided the house must be someone's cabin in the woods. Their get-away retreat from the hum drum of busy city life. No one would actually choose to live this way.

The girl, Ada, stared at us shuffling her feet.

"You got a TV?" said Sack breaking the silence.

Ada looked at him her expression odd. It was as if Sack had insulted her or something. I decided to change the subject. Her mother had just saved my life after all.

"How long you lived here?" I said as I sat up straight in the chair.

"Always," said Ada. "What's TV?" Obviously, she didn't want to change the subject.

I shrugged. "Ya know, TV — television — ya know…" Now I just sounded stupid. I had the strange feeling, especially given her quizzical expression, that she had no idea what I was talking about. "You watch shows on it. Get Smart. McHale's Navy. Bewitched —"

Ada's eyes widened. "Witches?" she said with a trace of fear in her voice.

I laughed sending a twinge of pain through my forehead, but it seemed to be less than before. Whatever Ada's mum had used on me seemed to be working. "No, silly. Not real witches. Make believe. TV…"

Ada continued to stare at me her gaze uncomprehending. I was about to give up when she said, "My Mamma's a witch."

Sack frowned. "Now who's making shit up. Yor Mom's a doctor. Yor mum's not a witch. There's no such things as witches. Everybody knows that."

Ada smiled, her eyes narrowing. "Momma fixed him," she said nodding toward me.

Sack shrugged. "Ya. I guess so…"

Now it's funny how you can see what people are thinking by looking in their eyes.

Right now Sack wasn't hiding anything.

"But if she's a witch then where's her broomstick?" I rolled my eyes at his obvious contempt for Ada's story.

Ada shrugged, obviously willing to shine Sack on. "She doesn't need one. She flies without one."

Sack laughed. "Ya right."

I decided I better step in before we got kicked out and had to walk across the forest. I was kinda hoping we could get a ride home.

"You got a car. We need a ride home before it gets dark. Our folks are gonna be worried."

Ada stared at me again as if I had an extra head growing from my shoulder. What planet did this girl live on?

I rolled my eyes. "A car. An auto-mobile. Truck. Bus. Something with wheels?"

Shem shook her head in wonderment. "Boy, you guys are sure weird. We don't have a wagon or even a horse." She tossed a sly look at Sack. "We don't need one."

Sack threw me a burning glare telling me he was through with being insulted. Sack wasn't the brightest marble in the bag but even he had feelings.

"So who lives here with you and your mom?" I said hoping at least keep to keep on her good side by making small talk.

Ada's gaze dropped to the floor and her face turned pink. I'd hit a nerve without meaning to. Oh shit.

"Huh…I'm sorry —"

"Just me and momma, now."

Sack must've noticed it to because he looked at me puzzled and slightly worried.

"Where's your dad?"

"He been hung."

Oh shit.

"Hung? For what?" said Sack. I shot nails at him for asking such an insensitive question.

"Poppa was a Negro. So they hung him."

Horrified I went quiet. We all went quiet, the only sounds came from the fireplace where wood crackled and popped. What do you say to something like that?

Like lightning from a clear blue sky, it dawned on me.

"Hold on. You're a liar. That kind of thing doesn't happen in Wisconsin —"

"Yes. It does," said husky female voice behind me.

Oh shit.

I froze. "Huh... sorry Mrs...uh, Mrs. Ada's mom...." Now I really sounded stupid.

Ada's mom came into view and sat in a chair opposite me. She reached over and wrapped her hands around mine. My heart leapt to my throat. She was gonna kill me.

"It's okay, Eddie," she said. As she said my name, I realized she hadn't asked me my name. But then how does she know me?

A tender smile crossed her lips. "Your great-grandfather was a Negro. That's why you're here."

I looked at her too stunned to speak. No. Horse shit. Impossible. Dad told me his grandfather was a farmer, born and bred in Beetown. What about mom? Realization hit me like a cold winter wind. Mom had never mentioned her grandparents. Not ever.

As if reading my mind the woman's grey eyes watched intent on my reaction. Being twelve at the time I'm sure she saw every conflicting emotion reflected in my face.

"It's OK, Eddie," she said again as if saying my name would drive the whirling confusion from my mind.

"Where is here?" I said at last.

Her dark eyebrows went up ever so subtly. "Why, Eddie don't you know? You're in Grant County, Wisconsin very close to same place you started. It's the turn of the century."

"Wow!" said Sack excitedly. "We're in the future!"

She shook her head. "No, dear Hubert (she used Sack's real name. A name he hated.) you're in the past. 1905 to be exact."

How could this be? Time travel was only in comic books or science fiction movies. And of course, the years were conveniently labeled so you didn't get lost like in the comic books. Then it struck me what had happened.

"The cave?" I said my mind whirling.

She nodded her eyes reflecting her pride in my ability to rationalize the situation like some adolescent Sherlock Holmes.

"Yes, Eddie. That's why it's called the Cave of Wonders."

"So ya mean, Huff is a ni — " I glared at Sack and he closed his mouth, but his eyes became hard as pebbles in a snow bank.

I knew at that moment I'd lost my best friend.

Cave of Wonders

***

After we left my great-grandmothers house we returned to 1966 via the cave. My life changed forever because of that day. A new path had been forged for my life and though I was twelve I somehow knew. I knew things wouldn't, couldn't be the same because we fell into that cave.

When we got home that day I said good-bye to Sack knowing I'd never see him again.

He died in 1971. After dropping out of high school he volunteered for the army. He was killed by a booby-trap in Vietnam two days after he arrived in that war.

My beloved grandmother died in the winter of 1967, those same sea-green eyes of the young girl from another time staring back at me as she passed from this life. I pray she found her promised land.

I went on to become a civil rights activist after the murder of Martin Luther King, and now work as an advocate for the NAACP.

It's a good life, a meaningful life. A life I never would have discovered had it not been for my grandmother and her Cave of Wonders.

Friends of a Warrior

The warm, humid breeze carrying the scent of dried grass, stale water, and ancient plains dust felt suddenly cool against the dark skin of my face. Only now the air carried with it the raw smell of blood, human blood.

I felt an unfamiliar knot of fear in the pit of my stomach and the razor thin sweeper blade in my right hand seemed heavier than before. My eyes were fixed on Jimmy Littlefeather who lay on his back in the warm sun. Jimmy's lifeless eyes were open and fixed on a single point in the golden hued sky that arched over my head. This should not have happened. Legod do not fear death....

I walked toward Jimmy's corpse, the golden strands of plains grass that rose around and over me were like an ocean of gold. The dry strands rustled off my leather hunting armor as they parted for me. When I neared my friend's body, I saw Jimmy's throat was ripped open by what could only be razor sharp teeth. Only one deadly predator could have killed Jimmy. A predator that was more dangerous than any wild animal on Earth.

Predators on Earth are normally fearful of humanoids. On Celestial II one predatory animal had never tasted human blood, because no human had ever been killed during the Kiowa Apache ritual hunts on this world.

Jimmy Littlefeather had honored me by inviting me on his first hunt. The hunt would prove Jimmy's warrior prowess and complete his journey to manhood.

Jimmy explained the first hunt of any Kiowa Apache's who came of age was a right of passage expected of all tribal warriors. The tribes of the Apache had been conducting the ritual hunts for centuries.

Father told me Legod's had a similar tradition and urged me to accept Jimmy's gift. He told me, "It's a great honor worthy of a Legod warrior."

For four months prior to leaving Earth, Jimmy and I practiced as a team until we knew each other's moves in our sleep. We practiced circling potential prey as if tightening a noose then, once we had maneuvered into position, we would practice closing in for the kill.

Jimmy was only allowed his Bowie knife and a bow and a quiver of arrows. I was allowed to carry my sweeper blade and matching, but shorter, dagger. My father had made the Legod weapons for me. I had trained with them day and night for weeks to prepare.

I also trained my body using the techniques my Karate and Kung Fu Sensei's taught me. While I am certain human fighting styles are not as good as Legod methods, I had little choice except to use human fighting styles until I learned more of the Legod ways.

Jimmy and I landed on the largest continent on Celestial II. The planet is a Galactic Empire nature preserve that requires permits and numerous inoculations, and waivers to gain permission for the ritual hunt.

The desert-like plains were in their early summer phase so we expected to find the animals near the many watering holes that dotted the landscape.

We hoped to hunt and slay one of the large antelope-like animals called a Deer-Leopard.

These were enormous creatures, with horns larger than an Earth moose, and mouths bursting with jagged sharp teeth designed to tear prey into bite size pieces. The average male stands twenty-five meters at the shoulder. They are large, fast predators capable of reaching speeds nearing one hundred kilometers per hour at a full gallop.

The Kiowa Apache named these fearsome beasts Those-That-Are-Fleet-of-Foot. Empire xenobiologists dubbed them Deer-Leopards.

A sudden sound met my ears causing me to freeze. Instinctively, gripping the handholds tight, I brought my sweeper blade to fighting position. I crouched lower in the tall grass and strained to hear any sound. A soft breeze coming from behind me meant I was upwind of the Deer-Leopard that killed my friend.

Maintaining a low crouch, a wall of swaying grass hiding me, I stepped sideways and began to work my way into a large curl formation like Jimmy and I had trained to execute. I would flank the beast hoping surprise it. No doubt my sudden appearance had momentarily startled the creature, causing it to temporarily abandon its fresh kill.

I moved quietly, my eyes darting back and froth, my senses alert for any sign that the tops the tall grass surrounding me were moving by more than the breeze.

I heard nothing. Until...I heard breathing. Heavy and nasal.

My olfactory senses detected the foul odor of rotting flesh and wet hair as the wind shifted to come directly at me. The beast was just ahead, probably not more then ten meters.

Good, I was up wind of the animal now. If I moved quickly I could be on it before it realized I was there. I would slice its throat open with the sharp blade of my sweeper. If the creature expected me, well... today is a good day to die.

I burst through the wall of grass in front of me with my blade raised to strike. I came to halt startled to see a large, pig-like animal, about the size of an Earth rhinoceros, standing calmly staring at me chewing a wad of grass.

This was no Deer-Leopard. This was a creature I had read about in my research known as a Rosairio. A placid herbivore that was friendly and harmless.

In fact, the researchers who wrote about the animal said the Rosairio bonded with humanoids much like a family pet might. I had a hard time picturing this drooling beast as a dog or a cat.

The Rosairio's large, watery blue eyes gazed at me with little interest registering behind them. It continued to chew the grass it had in its wide mouth.

Abruptly a loud sound came from the animal and the air was rendered with a foul stench that forced me pinch my nose between my fingers. Even breathing through my mouth filled my senses with the acidic odor.

"You are a filthy and foul smelling beast," I breathed glaring at the animal.

The Rosairio stopped chewing in mid-bite, his floppy white ears suddenly pulling away from the side of his bulbous head. I froze fearing the predator I hunted was about to leap upon me. After several seconds of silence, the Rosairio emitted a whimpering cat-like mew, turned and loped off moving away. The grass parted ahead of its bulky body as if the golden strands were being cleaved by an icebreaker. I watched in rapt fascination thinking the Rosairio might make a good watchdog after all, but at the same time relieved the beast was leaving.

It turned around to gaze at me; the blue eyes seemed to plead with me to follow it. I felt an odd sensation that I should follow it. As I had no idea where to start looking for my prey I decided I might as well follow the gentle creature.

I nodded and starting walking toward my new friend. "You better not continue to make such odors, beast or..."

What exactly I would do it if it continued to make such smells I did not know, but I decided if I was going to stay with this beast I required some form of protection.

I had a survival pouch with such items attached to my belt. A green and white handkerchief was inside mother had insisted I take with me. She said you never knew when you would need to blow your nose. At the time I had groaned inwardly, until father gave me a scathing look. Now I was glad I had it.

I pulled it out and tied it around my head covering my nose and mouth.

I did not recall reading anything about the Rosairio emitting odd smells. I suspected the noxious odor was a defense mechanism of some kind. Another of those substances humans liked to call one-hundred-percent-natural, like strychnine. Humans are so irrational sometimes. A Legod only thinks something kills or it does not. Simple. This odor did not kill, but long-term exposure would very likely cause a true Legod to kill the offender.

I had to pick up speed to keep up with the beast and was soon running through the sea of grass following the flattened path made by the creature.

I came to an abrupt halt when I came up on the Rosairio laying on its side a large feline-like animal sitting atop its belly. The cat emitted a deep growl, its yellow eyes warning me to stay away.

The cat was the size of a lion covered with light beige fur. Large glistening fangs protruded over its bottom lip. I moved slowly toward the fallen Rosairio the cats gaze fixed on my movements its shoulder muscles tensing as I came closer.

Gradually I raised my blade preparing for the attack I knew was coming, and braced my legs to spring into action.

The cat suddenly lunged at me, its massive sinewy bulk flying through the air, its paws tipped with what looked to be razor sharp nails fully extended. Just as it was about to land on me, I deftly stepped aside and brought the blade of my weapon down in a cutting motion with as much force as I could muster.

I heard a scream of pain and surprise. My vision went dark as something warm and sticky sprayed over me. The smell immediately told me I had made contact with the large cat.

I brought one hand up to clear my eyes of its blood. I needed to be able to see if I was going to counter another attack.

Looking about me, my body braced for an attack that I was certain would come; I was surprised to see the cat lying on its side blood flowing like a river from the creature's neck. My blow had been true.

I let my blade ease to my side as if it were dead weight, and turned to see the Rosairio had regained its feet the blue eyes excitedly staring at me. It looked positively giddy. I detest giddy.

I looked down at my hunting leathers and saw red blood covered me from my head to my feet. I must have severed a major artery.

Moving to stand over my kill, I noted the neck was nearly disconnected from the head, the neck having been cut clean through. I marveled at my prowess as a warrior. One day I would be the greatest warrior in my family house. Maybe even as great as our greatest warriors....

I was getting ahead of myself. There is nothing worse than a Legod warrior with a head swelled with pride.

I glanced back at the Rosairio whose body movements suggested it was anxious to continue after our prey. The enormous feet moved side to side like an impatient child.

I smirked and nodded. We must continue. Jimmy Littlefeather must be avenged.

***

An hour later the Rosairio, who I had taken to calling Spot, after a neighbor's dog back on Earth, and I exited the sea of grass at the edge clearing that abutted a forest. The air here was damp and smelled of wood rot and ferns, of which there were plenty spread beneath the tall blue-green trees.

The trees were set apart wide enough for even a Deer-Leopard so we could easily make out anything near the edge of the clearing. Unfortunately, twenty-five yards into the forest light could not penetrate so if predators were just beyond the edge of the light I would not be able to see them.

I looked at Spot and said, "Today is a good as any day to die."

The animal seemed to understand what I meant. Spot mimicked my earlier head motion and his blue eyes looked determined. Spot would make a fine Legod pet one day, but he could never replace my trill-beast I had as a child.

With Spot leading the way, we entered the forest. The temperature dropped several degrees and twigs snapped beneath my boots as we moved forward. Birds began to call to each other high in the trees tops.

This was not a stealthy mission that much was certain.

I gritted my teeth and walked forward keeping my blades handhold's gripped tight.

Suddenly, without warning, I felt a rushing sound coming from my left. I turned my head in time to see a dark shape just before it hit me.

The wind was knocked out of me as I felt my feet leave the ground and my blade leave my hands. I landed hard on my back with a grunt. I gasped for air and my body felt like one massive bruise.

A pair of large dark eyes appeared hovering over me and I realized I was looking into the unfeeling eyes of the Deer-Leopard. I felt its warm breath wash over me as it came closer. Then a low growl came from deep in its throat as the creatures mouth opened to reveal the twin rows of jagged bloodstained teeth. My head swam from the force of the blow and I imagined I could smell Jimmy's flesh. I knew I was looking at my death.

My mind swirled into a vortex of darkness as the world disappeared. When I awoke, I knew the next sight I would see would be heaven.

***

When my eyes fluttered open, I found myself staring into the friendly blue eyes of my father.

"Father? What are you doing in heaven?"

Father chuckled warmly, but his eyes revealed he was less than happy. He placed one hand behind my back and helped me sit up. On the other side of me was an Empire medical officer running instruments over my body.

I looked at father through the haze of my memory. "Jimmy…?" I said.

My father sighed and shook his head sadly. "No, Lotha, I'm afraid we found his body a kilometer from here…" He nodded toward the anti-gravity gurney with the sheet pulled over a hidden form that could only be Jimmy. "I'm sorry."

The last memory I had before I passed out hit me. "I should be dead…"

Father patted my shoulder. "It appears someone saved you by sacrificing themselves. " Father nodded over his left shoulder.

Helping me to stand, we walked with one of fathers arms supporting my weight, to the place where Spot lay on top of the Deer-Leopard.

It appeared Spot had somehow tackled the predator and broken its neck with the weight of his body.

Unfortunately, not before the Deer-Leopard slashed his throat with its sharp fangs. Spot bled to death saving me...

"There was the most awful smell when we arrived," said father.

"Yes. I know."

Father shook his head in wonderment. "I don't understand. This animal is a herbivore..."

I knew what I had to do. Letting go of father, my legs trembling, I moved to stand beside Spot. Placing one hand flat on his cooling flesh I raised my eyes skyward and emitted my best death scream.

Father watched me, his features locked in a puzzled expression, as I made my way to the gurney holding Jimmy's body and did the same for him.

Afterward I joined my father and the medical officer for the beam up to the waiting starship in orbit.

My father looked at me. "I understand Jimmy, but why the animal?"

As I felt the familiar tingle of the transporter beam just before we dematerialized I said, "They were both my friends, and both warriors."

Divided Loyalties

Lou Tubbs checked the clip in his blaster. The remaining energy was sufficient to do the job.

The wind on the other side of the windows of the rushing subway car howled in his ears nearly drowning out his thoughts. If he had, any doubts he needed to push that away. Flix MacKay was his friend, but his duty to The League of Scars took precedent. Fortunately, Flix wouldn't know what to expect. He thought two old friends were going to meet for lunch at the Arena café in Solar city. He would never suspect Lou was a ghost working on the fringes of the guard for his prince and his honor.

Once Lou had been a good solider, a good warrior...better than good really. He'd killed many men in battle until the day the general called him into his office. General Thomas told him he was going to take on a new assignment.

Ordered to sign a blood oath to the prince, he became the "clean up" man for The League of Scars. He would clean the house when called upon. The prince and his most loyal senior officers needed a ghost to exorcise the League of its demons.

Lou's honor forced him to agree even though he craved the rush of battle. The crushed and bloodied corpses beneath the steel feet of his battle mech were all he needed. That life was over.

His life changed.

For the past three years, he had been sent on missions of subterfuge. Missions to kill disloyal officers. Traitors and rapists. Cutthroats of every description. Knife. Blaster. Wire. These, coupled with stealth and deception, were his tools now.

Trouble was he felt naked when he killed. His battle mech was who he was yet now he scurried through dark alleys into the inky corners of every city and planet in the galaxy. No one was beyond the reach of his justice.

His life was a lonely one. His old brace mates shunned him. Trust is gone. He knew that one day his new life would catch up with him. One day…he pushes the thought away and shrugs, a shiver runs down his spine. No point in thinking about it.

He and Flix had been friends since they were children on New Anvil. Flix had once been a loyal soldier in the guard. And an exceptional warrior. Something must have gone wrong — very wrong with his old friend. The colonel never told him what happened. Not that it mattered. He was here to kill Flix no matter what the reason.

Flix had fled to Solar VII, which is why he was here. When he had contacted him Flix told him he was part of an established stable and that his patron had him fighting in the warrior arenas around the city. He said he was happy.

Lou's cover story was that he too had left the guard and fled to Solar VII to look for a stable to join. He asked Flix to meet him so they could discuss his newfound freedom.

For his part, Flix seemed pleased for him and seemed eager to help. When in doubt, lie. People were often more willing to accept a lie than the truth.

When Lou checked the local news net, he discovered that the press dubbed Flix MacKay a headhunter. He killed men and women in the arenas with no mercy or remorse. Gave no quarter. He'd racked up twenty-five kills in the year he'd been in Solaris city.

This conflicted with what Lou knew of his friend. Flix was no cold-blooded killer.

True he'd been a good solider, but to blindly kill his victims was something no honor bound warrior would do. And certainly not the Flix MacKay he knew.

The reconstituted eggs he had for breakfast again invaded his mouth. Nerves. Always happens just before a mission. He wondered how and why Flix had changed.

He holstered his blaster and studied the city that sped by outside the subway car. The collection of mold covered three story brick buildings and cracked sidewalks were indications of a sector headed on a downward spiral to slum. He would be happy when he got back to the clean air and shining cities of New Avalon.

Two more stops and he'd be on Canal Street. The city map at the hotel had said the café was two blocks from the subway station.

He studied his fellow passengers. A tough looking lot, who paid him no attention. Everyone was carrying their own blasters, laser pistols or projectile weapons so he wasn't unusual. Made it easier to blend in.

Finally, he arrived at the stop, disembarked and stood on the sidewall. He started down the street; his gray eyes studied the citizens who passed him. They were a sad looking lot.

Hardened men and women, many wearing black scuffed calf-length leather boots and heavy weapons hung from their hips. No one smiled or greeted each other. A sea of hard eyes and grim faces moved aside for him as he walked. They trudged by each other on a road to nowhere. He related to their plight. No one left Solar VII except in a pine box. That is if there was enough left to ship to their home planet.

Debts owed, fought, and died for. The gamblers slaves. The arenas claimed their victims and the few wealthy made a living off the bloody battles in the cities arenas.

No one made eye contact with him. Good thing. If anyone had, he might have been compelled to shoot first and ask questions later. You never knew when an enemy might appear.

In this line of work, your killer could be anyone, anywhere, anytime. You need eyes in the back of your head, or you were dead. He had survived fifteen attempts on his life in the time he had gone ghost. As odd as it sounds disloyal officers and murderers had friends or relatives who came to their aid when they discovered who Lou Tubbs was and what he was going to do. It seemed loyalty was a double-edged sword.

His knee still ached when it rained.

The air was stale and smelled of sweat and urine. A large rat scurried across the cracked sidewalk in front of him to disappear into a hole in the wall of a three-story walk up. No one but Lou seemed to take notice of the passage of the diseased rodent.

Nestled amongst the taller buildings that surrounded it he found the Arena café. It was located in a two-story red brick building at street level. Worn wood slats with large windows that faced the street framed the front of the café. He could see the round black glossy tables surrounded by cheap wood kitchen style chairs.

Only three tables contained customers, each with sandwiches or soup and heavy glass mugs of beer dripping with condensation from the cold beer meeting the humid air of the city. At the rear of the room, near the wall at the back, under a dim neon sign that advertised a local beer, sat Flix by himself. He had his own foam-topped mug of beer sitting in front of him.

Flix's blond hair, cut military style, was slicked down and glistened in the dim light. He wore the usual togs associated with freelance mech warriors. Tan cotton pants, a white shirt open at the collar, and a short black leather vest with matching black boots completed his ensemble.

A laser pistol hung off his hip in a brown leather holster. His eye scanned the other patrons. Lou knew this wasn't going to be easy.

Finally, Flix's dark eyes stopped on him and slow grin crossed his weathered features. There was a lot of mileage on that face. Lou hadn't seen Flix in a while but he looked older than Lou knew he was. It had been a long time.

Lou grinned easily and offered a short wave then pulled the door to the cafe open and went inside. His senses were assaulted by the greasy smells coming from the food. And his stomach protested by flipping slightly at the mixture of stale odors.

His booted feet slapped against the roughed hardwood floor as he walked to the table where Flix sat. Flix's eyes never left him, nor did the small grin and twinkle in his blue eyes dissipate. As Lou sat down Fix took a sip from his beer mug.

"Long time, 'ol buddy," said Flix.

Lou smirked and nodded as he sat down opposite his childhood friend. He removed his blaster from its holster and placed it on the table between them. Should he just do it now and get it over with? His heart felt heavy. They'd been boyhood pals. This was the hardest mission he'd ever undertaken. Honor. Loyalty. More than mere words.

Flix MacKay was disloyal. Flix MacKay had lost his honor. Only cowards ran away. He knew Flix MacKay must die.

He leaned back in the chair and felt the rounded dowels of the chair back press into him. The waiter, a balding man who must have weighed close to three hundred pounds, and who reeked of garlic, sweat and peppermint appeared. "May I get you something?" the man said in a small squeaky voice.

"I'll have what he's having," said Lou nodding at Flix.

The waiter disappeared and soon returned with a large glass mug of the strong beer. Lou needed to keep his wits about him until the job was done so he let it sit, the white foam churning and bubbling in the glass.

"Yup. Sure has Flix. I hear you're a real champion in these parts."

Flix shrugged and nodded. "Yeah. I'm pretty good."

Lou chuckled. "That's not the Flix MacKay I remember."

Flix smiled. "You're right, Lou. I'm the best there is." He frowned and his eyes became serious. "Problem with being king of the hill is everyone's gunning for you. And not necessarily in the arena."

He dropped one hand below the table and Lou knew Flix's fingers were resting on his laser pistol. No doubt an oft-practiced move.

This wasn't going to be an easy kill. Stealth wasn't the weapon of choice he would need. Surprise was what he needed.

"So why are you on Solar VII?" said Flix as his eyes narrowed.

Lou shrugged. "I don't like the way the rebellion's going. I don't trust The League of Scars, or the prince…"

"I don't recall you being interested in politics."

"I'm not. But I do so enjoy a good fight. Death before dishonor. Remember?"

Flix smirked and lifted his glass to his lips. He took a brief sip of the bitter beer. "Yeah. I remember." He placed the glass on the table where a ring of moisture had formed. "I also know where you fit in."

Lou reached for his blaster but before he could, he felt a knife blade pressing into the small of his back. He felt the warmth of someone's breath coming from behind him. He smelled cinnamon and cloves.

Flix wore a sloppy grin on his face. "Meet my wizard. Alice Trump."

A young raven-haired woman stepped from behind him a deadly long rapier in her slender pale right hand. "Nice to meet you," she said her voice husky, sexy and her ink black eyes sparkled with undisguised mirth.

They had him. Lou chastised himself.

What a fool he'd been. He was about to die and he knew it.

In a way, it was something he'd expected. Maybe even yearned for. Ever since that day in the general's office when he agreed to become a ghost he knew this day would come. Maybe it was his destiny. Should he at least try to make a show of it, or let nature take its course.

Lou reached again for his blaster but was too late. Sudden pain. He looked down. There in the center of his chest was the rapier's handle buried to the hilt. Funny, no blood.

"Kill or be killed. Isn't that what we do, Lou?" said Flix.

As the swirling darkness crept into the edges of his vision, Lou realized that Flix hadn't deserted his honor. All along this was a trap to rid the guard of a liability. Him. Flix MacKay would become the new ghost.

"Thank you…Flix," he whispered between dry lips.

Through blurred vision he saw Flix's puzzled expression.

"For what?" Flix's words echoed in his ears as he sagged to the floor landing in a heap as if he were a punctured balloon.

"No…divided…loyalties…" His voice dropped to a soft whisper then blackness took him. Flix and the rest of his world disappeared.

Only honor remained for Lou Tubbs.

About the Authors

International selling author, Russ Crossley writes romance under the name R.G. Hart, mystery/suspense under the name R.G. Crossley, and science fiction and fantasy under his own. This year there will be re-issues the romantic comedies, Bachelorette: Zombie Edition by Champagne Books, and Antique Virgin by 53rd Street Publishing, paranormal romantic comedy, Zomopolis, and a new western romance entitled, The Fire In Their Hearts co-authored with R.S. Meger will be published in 2013 by Champagne Books. Also, look for another Aloha adventure, Bloody Betty Queen of the Pirates coming in 2013 from Champagne Books.

In addition the near future suspense novel, The Last Serial Killer by R.G. Crossley was recently released by 53rd Street Publishing in ebook and trade paperback versions.

He has sold several short stories that have appeared in anthologies from Pocket Books, St. Matins Press, at Smashwords, Amazon, and other e-retail sites.

With his wife, romance author R.S. Meger, he owns and operates a small press publishing company, 53rd Street Publishing.

The company began in April 2011 and now has over one hundred e-book titles and a number of print titles, with more planned in 2012 and 2013.

He is a member of SF Canada and the Greater Vancouver Chapter of Romance Writers of America. He is also an alumni of the Oregon Coast Professional Fiction Writers Master Class taught by award winning author/editors, Kristine Katherine Rusch and Dean Wesley Smith.

To find a complete listing of his work check out his website http://www.rghart.com, http://russstory. blogspot.com.Razor's blog can be found at http://razorandedge.blogspot.com

Feel free to contact him on Facebook or Twitter. He loves to hear from readers

Other books by the Author

Titles as R.G. Crossley

Short Stories

Razor and Edge Mysteries
The Kidnapping of Billy Buttons
String of Pearls
Death by Clown
Beggin' For Murder
Ragged Ice
The Grand Central Mystery
A Strange Case of Undead Murder

Jazz Stiletto Mysteries
A Day Without Sunshine
Skullduggery

Non-Series Mysteries
Mirror Image
Dangerous Waters
Cape Disappointment
Boomerang
The Watcher of Wayburn Street
The Apprentice
Drip!
A Beautiful Friendship and The Parrot of Doom
Robine's Diary
The Christmas Club
Loose Ends

Splatter Pattern
It Takes Two

Anthologies
The Adventures of Razor and Edge:
Five Tales From The Quirky Detective Team

Novels
A Bad Case of Loyalty
The Last Serial Killer
Shear Murder

Titles as Russ Crossley

Novels
Attack of the Lushites
Revenge of the Lushites (coming soon)

Short Stories
Countdown
Shoeless Moe
Round Up At The Burger Bar:
The Story of Trixie Pug, Parts 1, 2, 3, 4, 5, 6, 7
Five Minutes
Blossom Queen, Barbarian
The Secret
The Family Line
End of the Flies
With Death You Get the Eggroll
The Penguin Sleeps With The Fishes
Only The Worthy
Hero For A Day

End of Empire
Strange Bedfellows
Big Business
A Perfect Crime
The Wise Guy and The Pirates
In Search of the Perfect Cup
T.I.N. Men
The Legend of G and the Dragonettes
The Incredible Mr. Fix-It
Lock Stock and Barrel
Divided Loyalties
Cave of Wonders
A Family Empire
Until We Meet Again
Dragon Rising

Presents Anthology Series
Five Tales of Urban Fantasy
Five Tales of Bizarre Detectives
Five Tales of Mystery and Suspense
Five Tales of Weird Fantasy
Spies, Detectives, & Heroes
Tales of Twisted Crime
Five Tales of The Unexpected
Tales From Space
10 by Russ Crossley
Round Up At The Burger Bar: The Story of Trixie Pug,
Parts 1- 5 The Beginning
Worlds of Science Fiction and Fantasy
More Tales of Mystery and Suspense
Ladies of the Jolly Roger
Justice Served

Titles as R.G. Hart

Short Stories
Tikka's Big Day
"My Partner the Zombie" —
Hungry For Your Love Anthology
(St. Martin's Press)
Big Hairy Deal
One Red Shoe
A Bad Day in Lunden Texas
Hook Island
Grind Manor
Bloody Betty, Queen of the Pirates (coming soon from
Champagne Books)

Novels
Bachelorette: Zombie Edition
(from Champagne Books)
Antique Virgin
The Fire In Their Hearts
with R.S. Meger (coming soon from Champagne
Books)
Zomopolis

www.ingramcontent.com/pod-product-compliance
Lightning Source LLC
Chambersburg PA
CBHW030545130626
46552CB00006B/2428